For my son, Isaac, who has spoken
Spanish for me when I needed it.
—K. E.

To Carolyn, Empress of English.
—E. O. S.

Speak English for Us, Marisol!

WRITTEN BY Karen English

ILLUSTRATED BY Enrique O. Sánchez

Albert Whitman & Company

Library of Congress Cataloging-in-Publication Data
English, Karen.
Speak English for us, Marsol! / by Karen English;
illustrated by Enrique O. Sánchez.
p. cm
Summary: Marisol, who is bilingual, is sometimes overwhelmed when her
Spanish-speaking family members and neighbors need her to translate for them.
ISBN 0-8075-7554-2 (hardcover)
[1. Spanish language—Fiction. 2. Hispanic Americans—Fiction.]
I.Sánchez, Enrique O., 1942-   ill. II. Title.
PZ7.E7232 Sp 2000
[E]—dc21
00-008312

The illustrations were painted in gouache and acrylic.
The text typeface is Maiandra GD.
The design is by Scott Piehl.

M arisol is running home from school—down Valencia, up Presidio, over to Euclid Parkway. Marisol is in a big hurry today. Luisa might be having her kittens, and Marisol wants to be there. Then…

"Marisol!" Uncle Tomás calls from his poultry shop. "Oh, Marisol!
Where are you going so fast? I need your help."

Marisol stops and looks up into his round, smiling face with the
big twirly mustache. "Hola, Uncle."

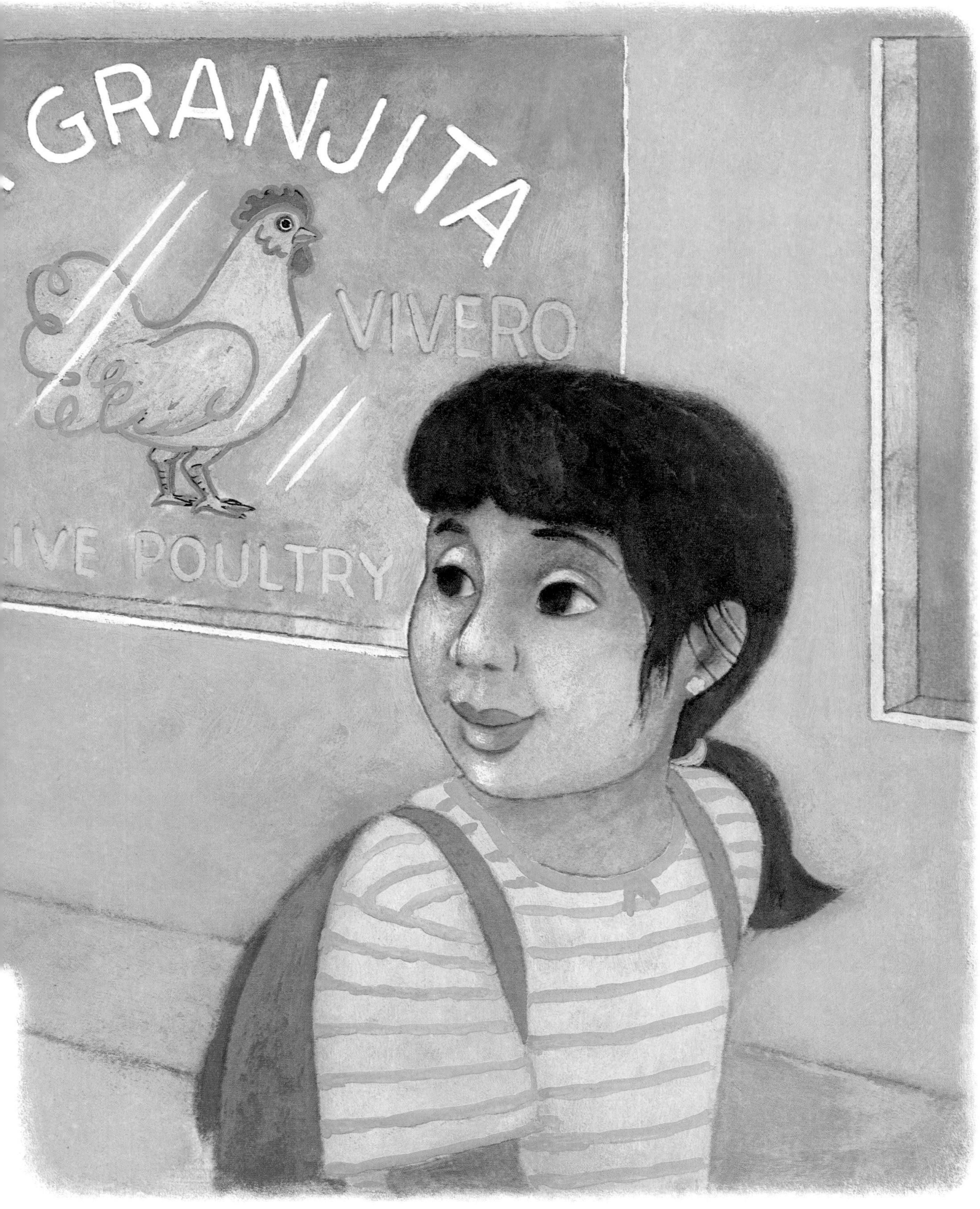
GRANJITA
VIVERO
LIVE POULTRY

"Come with me," he says, leading her out to the alley where the poultry man waits by his truck. "Por favor," Uncle tells her. "That man does not understand Spanish."

"Sí, Uncle. What do you want me to tell him in English?"

"I want you to say his prices are too high. Tell him his brother is much more reasonable. Tell him he's stubborn."

"Oh, Uncle, I can't tell him all that."

Instead, Marisol says, "Mister, my uncle needs the chickens at the old price or he will buy them from someone else."

The man shrugs. Then he unloads the chickens.

"What did you say?" Uncle asks.

"What you said, sort of."

"Gracias, Marisol! You can be on your way. Oh, take a chicken for your mother."

  Now Marisol is running again. She doesn't want to be running carrying a whole plucked chicken, but she has to get home to Luisa before the kittens come.

  Down Mareno with the jacarandas in bloom. Up June Street where the library is. She reaches Porter Avenue, her own street. Then . . .

  "Oh, Marisol!" It's Auntie Flora calling from her upstairs window.

  "Sí, Auntie."

"I need your help!" Auntie comes down and leads Marisol up the stairs. "You need to talk to the furniture store lady. You need to tell her they must have sent my couch to the wrong address."

Marisol sighs deeply.

"You tell them I need that couch today. Your cousin's bridal shower is on Saturday, and we'll only have my hard kitchen chairs to sit on. I already gave my old couch to Mrs. Morgan. I can't ask for it back!"

"Sí, Auntie." Marisol picks up the telephone receiver and hears music. "You're on hold, Auntie."

After a long time, the lady returns. "Please tell your aunt that her couch is scheduled to be delivered tomorrow at noon. Not today."

"Yes, ma'am." Marisol turns to Auntie. "Auntie, your couch is coming tomorrow—not today."

"Oops! You go on your way, Marisol. Gracias. Take this bread I baked for your mother."

SAN RAMON VALLEY UNIFIED SCHOOL DIST.
ALAMO ELEMENTARY SCHOOL
1001 WILSON ROAD
ALAMO, CA 94507

Now Marisol is running home with a loaf of bread and a chicken. She turns into her front yard.

"Oh, Marisol! What took you so long? I need your help to fill out my application forms. Can you come up?" It's Mrs. Lopez calling from the building next door.

"Sí, Mrs. Lopez." Marisol sighs again as she heads up the stairs.

Mrs. Lopez has Marisol's favorite drink, strawberry horchata, waiting for her.

"Here's the application," Mrs. Lopez says, spreading it out on the table. "There's no Spanish on the back, so I can't understand it. I need to fill it out right so I can take a class at the college."

It takes two glasses of horchata before Marisol has finished helping Mrs. Lopez.

"Gracias, Marisol," Mrs. Lopez says as Marisol runs down the stairs.

Now Marisol can look under the porch to see if Luisa has had her kittens.

But her front door flies open and Mamá is saying, "Hurry! Come with me!"

"Where?"

"To the telephone company. They sent me the wrong bill, and now they say they're going to cut off our phone by the end of today!"

It's a long walk to the telephone company.

There's a long line to stand in there. Marisol is tired. Everyone in the line looks sad and tired.

"You tell the lady I won't pay someone else's bill."

"Sí, Mamá."

"It's not fair."

"Yes, *okay*."

Finally they reach the counter. The lady looks tired, too. Marisol explains about the bill that belongs to someone else. The lady takes the bill out of Marisol's hand, squints at it, then leaves the counter. When she comes back, she explains that it has been taken care of.

All the time Mamá is saying, "¿Qué, qué?" in Marisol's ear. After the lady is finished, Marisol gets to explain everything.

On the way home, Mamá says, "I need to stop by the market for vegetables to go with Uncle's chicken."

Marisol gives another sigh. Mamá can never go to just one place.

"It won't take long. I want to make a nice dinner for your father."

But it does take long, and they don't leave the market until twilight, though twilight is nice—with Mamá.

At last they're home, and Marisol gets to do what she's been
waiting to do all day. She shines Papi's flashlight under the porch.
Luisa—alone—rests peacefully. No kittens yet.

Just then, from inside, it's, "Oh, Marisol! Come here quick!"

Oh, no—what now? Marisol thinks.

"I want to show you something from my English class," Mamá says. "Test me."

"Sí, Mamá."

Marisol takes the book. "Good morning, Mrs. Garcia. How are you?"

Mamá looks at Marisol tenderly. She speaks the English words carefully. "I am fine, thank you, because I have a wonderful daughter named Marisol. She is the best daughter a mother could have. She helps everyone."

"That's not in the book," Marisol says.

Mamá smiles. "No, it isn't," she says, "but it's in my heart."